FRASER VALLEY REGIONAL LIBRARY

39083501253455

Racing for Diamonds

ORCA
YOUNG
READERS

Racing for Diamonds

Anita Daher

ORCA BOOK PUBLISHERS

Text copyright © 2007 Anita Daher

All rights reserved. No part of this publication may be reproduced or transmitted in any form or by any means, electronic or mechanical, including photocopying, recording or by any information storage and retrieval system now known or to be invented, without permission in writing from the publisher.

Library and Archives Canada Cataloguing in Publication

Daher, Anita, 1965-

Racing for diamonds / written by Anita Daher.

(Orca young readers)
ISBN 978-1-55143-675-3

I. Title. II. Series.

PS8557.A35R33 2007 jC813'.6 C2006-907059-8

First published in the United States, 2007
Library of Congress Control Number: 2006939251

Summary: All Jaz's new-found skills as a Junior Canadian Ranger are put to a life-and-death test.

Orca Book Publishers gratefully acknowledges the support for its publishing programs provided by the following agencies: the Government of Canada through the Book Publishing Industry Development Program and the Canada Council for the Arts, and the Province of British Columbia through the BC Arts Council and the Book Publishing Tax Credit.

Typesetting by Christine Toller
Cover artwork by Glenn Bernabe
Author photo by Paul Norbo

ORCA BOOK PUBLISHERS
PO Box 5626, STN. B
VICTORIA, BC CANADA
V8R 6S4

ORCA BOOK PUBLISHERS
PO Box 468
CUSTER, WA USA
98240-0468

www.orcabook.com
Printed and bound in Canada.
Printed on 100% PCW paper.
10 09 08 07 • 4 3 2 1

For Taco and Squirrel

Acknowledgments

My deepest gratitude to all the people and organizations that helped in the research and assembly of this adventure: my insightful editor, Sarah Harvey; the Manitoba Arts Council; Canadian North; the kids and staff at Mackenzie Mountain School; the Norman Wells Historical Society; Liz and Nick Dale; Judith Drinnan; Kidcritters Helene, Marina, Marsha, Janet, Elizabeth, Rose, Chris, Mary, James and Christine; and the Canadian Rangers, especially Tony, Conrad, Ted, Sweet Daddy George, Rick, Floyd, Dave and Major Chris.

Out of respect and affection I have pasted several real names of folks (and dogs) onto characters who are entirely fictional.

The Canol Trail is real and has a significant place in Canadian and American history. The race in this story follows the real trail up to a point; however, I have taken some liberties with the geography. Anyone wishing to hike the trail should heed the US military's civilian trail worker recruitment poster from 1942: *This is no picnic!*

Chapter One

"For crying out loud, Jaz, would you drop it already?"

Colly looked like he was about to explode. Jaz could almost see the steam spewing from his ears, and his eyes were shooting lightning bolts. Blue eyes. That was all Jaz had asked him about. After all, Colly had said that his people were Dene. Up until two months ago, Jaz had lived her whole life in Yellowknife, in the Northwest Territories. In Yellowknife there were people of many different cultures—Dene, Inuk, East Indian, Scottish, Korean, French, German and more—but she'd never met a Dene boy with blue eyes before.

"Why so touchy?" she asked, tucking a stray curl from her short red mop behind her ear. She was not at all put off by his anger, even though his shout echoed in the belly of the old warehouse that served as their Junior Canadian Ranger barracks.

"Well, I don't know, Jaz. Maybe it's because you have my arm wrapped up with my leg and I can't move!"

Oops. It was true. Colly had become a tangled-up mess of green Junior Ranger sweatshirt, white bandage and purple angry-face.

Jaz had been with the Junior Canadian Rangers—JCRs for short—for just a month, ever since she'd turned twelve on January 15 and become old enough to join. But if she was going to be ready for the sled-dog derby planned for mid-March, she had to get better at basic first aid. If she didn't get it right, she wouldn't be allowed to go, and she desperately wanted to. Teams from all the JCR patrols from the Northwest Territories would be competing in pairs, and the top three teams would get to go to Ottawa for Canada Day.

Destiny, Jaz's new home, was a nice enough place, but it wasn't nearly as exciting as Ottawa. True, Destiny wasn't all that far away from Yellowknife, which could be pretty exciting, but there was no road in or out. You could only get to it by bush plane, or, in winter, over the ice on Great Slave Lake. Destiny was small, but there was still plenty to do, even if it didn't have city things, like Internet cafés or an indoor swimming pool. In Destiny, if she wanted to swim she'd have to go jump in the lake—something she felt like telling Colly to do, and often!

"Why don't you like me?" she asked, rocking back on her sneaker heels.

"Why are you asking me that?" Colly snapped, struggling to free himself from the gauze.

"Because I want to know."

"I don't NOT like you!" he said. "But, man, did anyone ever tell you that you ask a lot of questions?"

She grinned. "As a matter of fact, yes."

He took a deep breath and let it out slowly, looking to the ceiling as if for help. Jaz noticed his eyes were a lighter blue than her own, almost like ice. Curious.

"Are you part albino or something?" she asked.

"Just fix this, and wrap me up right!"

Okay, so maybe Colly didn't NOT like her, she thought, pulling bits of sticky tape from her fingers, but it was no secret that they were about as good together as potatoes with strawberry sauce. This wouldn't be so bad, except that Colly, only one year older than Jaz, was a master corporal who outranked her in their Junior Ranger patrol. Jaz hated him bossing her around.

Aside from having to put up with Colly, being a JCR rocked! When they were on patrol, or helping elders in their community, or even just listening to Sergeant

Sugar talk, she didn't miss her friends in Yellowknife quite so much. It was different from a cadet program: JCRs were more relaxed and informal. They even called their commanding officers by their first names, and there wasn't a lot of marching or saluting or saying "Sir." Sergeant Sugar's real name was Bobby Lemons, but he told everyone to call him Sugar so he wouldn't be such a sourpuss. He was just joking. Sergeant Sugar was about as sour as cotton candy.

She was excited about learning the kind of on-the-land survival skills that might save someone's life someday. The Rangers—the adult ones—were called on to help people who got into difficulty in the harsh terrain of the Northwest Territories. She also liked how they were learning traditional skills from the elders, like how to make medicines from plants. During their weekly meetings, Sergeant Sugar talked a lot about respect and healthy lifestyles. Dog-mushing through the mountains of the western Northwest Territories would be *very* healthy!

"Is there a problem, Colly?"

Jaz looked up from her rats' nest of gauze to see Sergeant Sugar standing over them. His red Ranger sweatshirt was surrounded by a forest of green as the other Junior Rangers, all eighteen of them, silently gathered around Jaz and Colly. She didn't know why. It's not like they were really bleeding or fighting or anything. Well, not exactly.

"No problem, Sergeant Sugar," Colly answered.

"How is Jaz doing? Will she be ready for the derby?"

"No problem," he said again.

As Sergeant Sugar moved on to check some of the other bandaged pairs, Jaz figured she'd better say thanks. After all, Colly didn't have to stick up for her. Would she have done the same for him?

"I know I kind of suck at this," she said. "But I'll be ready, I promise."

"Make sure you are!" he said, flinging the bandages in a pile and standing up. "And practice on someone else!"

"Anyone?" she asked the group, grinning. "Come on, two wraps for the price of one!" Shelby, a JCR who had been with the group for ages, laughed and offered the arm not already bandaged by someone else. "Why do you and Colly always argue?" she asked.

Jaz shrugged. "I guess because he's always getting things wrong."

It was true that she and Colly were often at odds, which sometimes annoyed the rest of the group, who didn't see the point of whatever they were arguing about. But she didn't NOT like him either. It was just that...well, she didn't know why they didn't get along. Sometimes people were just like that.

Take her mom and dad, for instance. Before their divorce two years ago, they argued all the time. They'd argued so much that most people weren't very surprised when they split up. Since then, Mom and Dad had agreed on almost everything. Mom traveled a lot for her job, so it was decided that Jaz should stay in Yellowknife with Dad and visit her mother as often as it fit into all their schedules. Jaz missed her mom, but she was relieved when the arguing stopped. Life had been almost great...until last summer, that is.

The months between grades five and six had been spent at her dad's fishing lodge at Hidden Lake, just like the summer before. Last summer, however, she'd had an adventure involving grizzly bears, and she got lost in a network of caves underneath a mountain. Right after that, she and her dad had moved from Yellowknife to Destiny.

Everything might have been okay, except that after Jaz's run-in with the grizzly bears, her mom began to worry, and the worry turned into arguments with Dad. Why did they have to argue? She hated it! They argued about everything. Worst of all, it was all her fault. She thought she knew how to fix it, though. If she won the derby and proved that she had amazing outdoor skills, Mom and Dad would forget the grizzly bears, and the arguing would stop.

"Earth to Jaz," Shelby was saying. "Welcome back. I think you're finished."

With some surprise, she noticed the other girl's arm was properly bandaged. Huh. She must have done that when she wasn't paying attention. No sweat. Maybe sometimes when you thought about things too much, you just tied yourself—and other people—in knots.

She noticed Colly watching her, but was unable to read his expression. Master corporal or not, he made her want to pop a balloon right behind him when he wasn't expecting it. Instead she stuck out her tongue. Some things just had to be done, never mind rank.

Chapter Two

Inside the old green warehouse, the JCRs were buzzing.

"Did you hear the news?" Shelby asked. "A diamond polisher has gone missing from Yellowknife."

"No kidding? What happened to him?" Jaz asked.

"Nobody knows, but anytime something happens at a diamond company, everyone gets in a big panic."

It was true. Ever since companies had started digging up diamonds in the Northwest Territories a few years back, the world seemed to have caught diamond fever. News reports said Canadian diamonds were the best anywhere. That meant big business for Yellowknife, the territory's capital.

Two short blasts of a whistle silenced the buzz.

"Listen up, JCRs!" Sergeant Sugar called as the Junior Rangers whispered and shoved their way into couches and chairs at one end of the room. "We're going over to Joe Huffam's place to practice hooking up dogs to a sled. Some of you already know how to do this, but even if you do, you might have picked up some bad habits. Be respectful and listen closely. You might learn something that will help you succeed on the Canol Trail."

A portion of the Canol Heritage Trail near Norman Wells would be the site for the Northwest Territories JCR derby. Norman Wells was just south of the Arctic Circle, about a ninety-minute flight northwest from Yellowknife.

"Yeah!" Jaz exclaimed, punching the air. "Oh… sorry, Sergeant Sugar. I'm listening, really."

The JCRs surrounding her giggled. All except Colly, who shot her a stern look.

Sergeant Sugar smiled. "We're all excited, Jaz. But make sure you listen, even when you don't think you need to. That way you won't miss anything, and I think we all know that you don't like missing anything!"

All the JCRs laughed this time, even Colly.

Parka back on, Jaz tromped along the trail beside Shelby and George, with Colly just behind. Joe's place wasn't far, but then again, nothing was far in Destiny. As she hiked two blocks past the post office and up over the hill past the cemetery, Jaz could already hear the dogs.

"Tell me more about the diamond polisher," she said, looping her arm inside Shelby's.

"It's all over the radio and TV," Shelby said.

"Missed it, I guess."

"It was a guy named Gunther Wegener," George said, throwing a snowball at a telephone pole. He hit it, but that was no surprise. Next to Colly, George had the best aim. He was always talking about how he'd been hunting with his dad since he was four and how he could hit anything he could see.

She stopped walking. "Are you sure, George? I know Gunther."

Others began crowding around her, asking questions.

"You know the missing guy?"

"Is he your dad's friend?"

"How do you know Gunther Wegener?"

"What do I have to do to keep you guys moving?" Colly exclaimed, pushing Jaz forward.

"Who peed in your pudding?" Jaz asked.

"Just go!" Colly yelled.

Jaz glanced ahead and saw Joe's weathered cabin nestled into a hill alongside three brightly painted sheds and a dozen or more doghouses. The cabin was squat and leaned to one side. It looked old. How long had it been there? Jaz knew that 150 years ago Destiny had been a fur-trading post. That only lasted for about forty years, but even after the trading stopped, some families stayed. Over time a few more joined them. It was quiet and a good place for people who wanted to live off the land but still be close to a bigger center.

The tour company that her dad worked for had decided that Destiny was a perfect place for a new winter lodge. Guests could snowshoe, try dogsledding and view the aurora borealis far away from city lights and noise and still get back to Yellowknife quickly when it was time to go. Because her dad had experience with his own summertime fishing lodge, the company asked him to manage the new lodge.

It also helped that he had his own airplane. He could fly in tourists, and once in a while he picked Mom up in Yellowknife and flew her in to Destiny for a barbecue.

As if on cue, Jaz's stomach growled. No growling from the dogs, though. As soon as all the JCRs had arrived and gathered around Joe, the happy beasts started jumping around, straining at the ends of their ropes, yipping and crooning. Sled dogs loved their jobs. They made you believe that pulling a sled was the best thing in the world. Maybe it was, but Jaz couldn't wait to be mushing along behind one! She tried to tuck away her questions about what exactly had happened with Gunther, but they wouldn't quite go away. She knew Gunther. Besides being a diamond polisher, he owned a café she and her dad liked to visit. She licked her lips at the thought of Gunther's yummy hot apple strudel. Every Wednesday he would time it so that it was fresh from the oven when she stopped by after school. He would give her a small slice for free, telling her she was "taste testing" it for him.

One day Jaz asked, "Where did you learn to bake apple strudel?"

"My mother taught me," he said.

"When you were in Germany?"

"Yes," he said. "That is where I grew up. Since you like strudel so much, maybe one day I will teach you. Yes?"

"Yes, please!"

Whenever Gunther wasn't in the café, he was hiking back and forth to the diamond-polishing facility, always smiling, tapping his trademark green flat-cap and wishing folks a very good day. His routine was so regular it was almost boring. How could he go missing?

She shook her head, chiding herself for missing what Joe was talking about. She breathed deeply, taking in a snootfull of wet doggy smell mixed with the wood smoke that curled from the cabin's chimney. Joe was holding the collar of a white husky he called Salty. She was twisting this way and that, black lips spread into what looked like an open-mouthed grin, tongue lolling out the side.

"Sled dogs have always been important to the northern way of life," Joe began.

Rowfff!

"You see? Salty is trying to tell us how important she is."

Laughter filled the yard, which seemed to please Salty even more.

Joe showed them the harness and how it attached to the towline, which connected all the dogs to the sled. As soon as Salty was attached, she settled down, ears forward, mouth still open. She looked as if she knew what was coming and was happy about it, but was willing to wait...for a little while, anyway.

Joe took another dog by the collar.

"This is Oscar. Who would like to attach him to the sled?"

Jaz's hand shot up. "Me! Me! Oh please, pick me!"

"Okay, Jaz, no need to be shy," he said, laughing.

Jaz held Oscar by the collar and clamped her legs on either side of what she figured must be the dog's waist. It wasn't easy, because Oscar was wagging his tail so hard that his whole body was wagging with it!

"You've got him tight. Now, slip the harness over his head."

She did.

"Now lift each of his legs through. Good. Is the harness nice and snug?"

"I think so. What if it's too tight?"

"It's not. Just make sure his skin isn't bunched up anyplace it shouldn't be. Remember what comes next?"

With a satisfying snap-snap, Jaz connected Oscar to the towline and stepped back.

"Are we going to go for a ride today, Joe?"

"Of course!"

**

While the JCRs took turns hooking up the dogs and riding around Joe's property, Jaz thought of nothing but fun, snow and racing. When she got back to the

JCR quarters, however, she could wait no longer. "T
me from the beginning, Shelby. What happened to
Gunther?"

Shelby filled her in with a little help from George.
Apparently after working on a batch of diamonds,
Gunther had signed out for the day. When he didn't
open up his café the next morning and didn't answer
his phone, his staff got worried and called the police.

"What did the police say?"

"Nothing, at first."

"What do you mean?" Jaz asked.

"The police said he wasn't officially a missing
person. But when the diamond company said that he
hadn't returned the diamonds he was working on, it
caused a huge fuss."

"He's a thief!" George said.

"He is not!" Jaz cried.

"Jaz is right, George," Shelby said. "There were no
diamonds missing. It was just a mistake. The paperwork was wrong."

"On the radio they're saying it's suspicious," Colly
said, setting aside the *How to build an emergency air-
strip* instruction sheets he'd been passing out. "Look,
the guy has his hands on millions of dollars worth of
gems every day. Maybe he got greedy, took some and

…n disappeared. Maybe he tried to cover it up with …e paperwork, but the company still noticed something was wrong."

"That's just stupid!" Jaz cried.

"I'm just saying it *could have* happened, Jaz. On the radio they're saying the RCMP Diamond Squad is looking into it. Why the Diamond Squad instead of the regular police? They must have a reason."

Feeling heat rise in her cheeks and neck, she could barely make her thoughts wait in line so that they would come out one at a time.

"Maybe they're just looking into the paperwork because that's what they do—you don't know! Maybe he fell down somewhere and got hurt. Maybe he went out of town and didn't tell anyone…"

"And maybe you're just mad because you don't want to admit you could be wrong about him," Colly finished for her.

"Grrr!" Jaz felt like her head was going to pop off. She would have said something more, except Sergeant Sugar stepped in.

"Right, you two," he said. "Is there a problem here?"

"Just another fight," Shelby said, rolling her eyes. "They're always fighting about something."

Sergeant Sugar looked from Colly to Jaz, then back to Colly. "Colly, Jaz, please stand at attention."

Jaz straightened, facing Sergeant Sugar, heels together and arms straight at her sides. Out of the corner of her eye she could see Colly do the same.

"What value do we hold above all others in this patrol, Colly?"

"Respect," Colly mumbled, dropping his chin.

"Do you respect Jaz's opinions?"

"Sure I do," he said. "But she's wrong about that diamond polisher. The guys on the radio wouldn't have said it was suspicious if there wasn't something to it. Just my opinion."

"Jaz, do you respect Colly's opinion in this matter?"

"Nope."

"What was that?"

"I said, 'Nope,' Sergeant Sugar. You always say it's important to be honest. I don't care what Colly heard on the radio. The radio is wrong, and so is he."

Sergeant Sugar frowned and addressed the group. "JCRs, do we also agree that cooperation is important to our unit?"

"Yes, Sergeant!" they cried.

"Fine. It's decided then."

"What?" Colly and Jaz said together.

"You two will be partners in the derby. If you want to win, you'll find a way to cooperate and respect each other's honest opinions."

Suddenly the day didn't feel quite so bright and happy.

Chapter Three

"It's good, Mom. I mean, it took a while to get used to it, but I like Destiny."

"I'm glad, Jaz," Mom said, her voice crackling over the phone. Bad connection. "But you know cities offer quite a few more opportunities. Maybe we can find a way for you to stay with me in Edmonton."

Her heart jumped. Even though Mom visited lots and called her on the phone every couple of days, Jaz still missed her. She missed hugs that smelled like coconut, and just hanging out, watching movies and eating popcorn.

She didn't know what to say, and that was weird. Talking about stuff wasn't usually a problem for her. This was different, though, maybe because it was so important. Mom and Dad were always arguing about it. They hadn't told her that in so many words, but she'd overheard her dad say a few things, and sometimes when he handed her the phone after talking to her mom, he would be rubbing his neck. He did that when he was upset.

How did that saying go? If you don't know what to say, try saying something else. That wasn't exactly right, but it was close enough.

"I love you, Mom."

"I love you too, Jaz."

Jaz hung up the phone and looked at her dad. After handing over the phone and then making Jaz a batch of buttermilk pancakes for breakfast, her father had dozed off in his chair at the kitchen table, his head resting against his folded arms. No surprise, really. He'd taken a group of Japanese tourists out to look at the northern lights the night before and hadn't gotten back until well after midnight. The tourists were still sleeping, but their bright red parkas were hanging on hooks by the door with their white moon-boots neatly lined up underneath. Tiny puddles of water from melted snow were spreading out, making one big pool.

Jaz pulled out the mop and wiped up the mess while her dad snoozed on. She enjoyed the tang of pine in the cleaner and the way the ammonia pinched her nose. Quietly she returned the mop to the closet and neatly realigned the boots.

Dad would have told her not to bother, that he could do it. Since their move to Destiny, he'd hardly asked her to do anything. Sometimes she wished he would. Most days it felt like he didn't need her help at all. Mom, on the other hand, could probably use her help.

Still, if she weren't here, who would Dad play checkers with? And what would he do with all those tiny green marshmallows he bought last Halloween for their special Dad 'n' Jazy Super Spinach Marshmallow Salad? That treat was only for her and her dad—never for the tourists.

A blast of static from the radio caught her attention. What she heard next held it.

"Wake up, Dad!" she cried, shaking him. This was too important for him to sleep through.

"Wha…?"

"It's quite the mystery, Phil," the guy on the radio was saying.

"Dad, please wake up and listen!"

"Okay, Jaz," he said, rubbing his eyes, "I'm listening."

"Something is definitely fishy, Randy. The paper-work was messed up, which is why the company sounded the alarm. But when they checked their inventory there was nothing missing."

"Gunther?" Her dad sounded groggy, but he was awake. "Right. That's all anyone is talking about."

"Shhh…let's listen!" she said, scraping her chair closer to the radio.

"…I know the guy, Randy—so do you. Most of us have had a bowl of homemade soup at Wegener's Place at one time or another."

"I especially love the cheesy onion-potato soup, Phil. Have you had it? It's terrific with fresh bannock."

"Well, there you go, Randy."

"There what goes, Dad?" Jaz cried, turning to him. "They didn't tell us anything!"

"Patience, Jaz. The news is coming on now."

They listened, but Jaz didn't hear any answers to the questions that were bunching up in her brain. "Forget the mixed-up paperwork, what happened to Gunther?"

Dad shrugged. "Maybe he went away for a vacation. I'm sure they would be making more of a fuss if they really thought he was missing. Probably just another mix-up."

Jaz frowned. They shouldn't have said he was missing in the first place if they weren't planning on telling them the rest of it.

But what if Gunther really was missing and the Diamond Squad was keeping it hush-hush? What if he was secretly working for them, maybe as an undercover agent?

A rap on the door interrupted her musing.

"Hey, Mr. Kelly," Colly said, stamping the snow off his boots before pulling them off and hanging up his coat. He was carrying a small stack of folded paper.

"Are these the maps?" Jaz asked, taking them from him and setting them on the table.

She tried to sound cheerful, but she still wasn't happy about partnering with Colly, and she didn't think he was too thrilled about it either. They'd tried to talk Sergeant Sugar out of it, but he wouldn't budge. If they were going to win this thing, they'd have to do it together.

"Pretty exciting stuff, racing along the Canol," Dad said. "Not even experienced hikers attempt it much in the summer, and no one tries it in the winter."

"We're only racing through the first part, Mr. Kelly, just to the end of Dodo Canyon." He flipped open a map and pointed to a part he'd highlighted. The rest of the trail showed up as a dashed line all the way through the Mackenzie Mountains to the Yukon. "It's safe enough. The rivers should be frozen this time of year."

"I have no doubt, Colly. Still, I'm glad you'll be looking out for my girl. She does have a nose for trouble."

Jaz rolled her eyes. "Come on, Dad. My nose is for getting *out* of trouble!"

"Okay, you've got me there," Dad said, laughing. He looked to Colly, who wasn't laughing. "Smile! I was only teasing."

"Okay," Colly said, but he didn't sound too sure.

He probably missed her dad mumbling "Mostly teasing" into his hand as he turned away, still chuckling. Jaz heard it though. Her ears were every bit as good as her nose.

"I'll leave you kids to it, then," he said, clearly this time. "I need a proper nap before my guests wake up."

With a nod, he climbed the narrow back stairs that led from the kitchen to their family quarters.

"So I guess you heard the news?" Colly asked, flattening the first map with his palm.

"You mean about Gunther? Yeah, but they're not really telling us anything."

"They're telling us all they know, Jaz. It sounds like your friend is in the clear, anyway."

"He's not my friend. I just know him, okay?"

"Okay, whatever. I only wanted to say I'm sorry I called him a thief. Obviously I was wrong."

Jaz sat back and looked at Colly, who was busy with the map and definitely not looking back at her. On purpose, Jaz thought. This is where her mother would say *Take the high road, Jaz,* which really meant *Don't rub it in.* The thing is, she had nothing to rub.

"I guess we don't really know what happened, or why the paperwork was messed up, or where Gunther went," she said. "I mean, it sounds like something fishy did happen. We just don't know what."

"They'll figure it out."

"Yeah...probably."

Truce on the table, along with the map, they got to work. Something else they'd agreed on was that they wanted to know the route inside out and backward. True, it would be groomed before they got there, but they would be racing for about two hours between each checkpoint, and weather could be unpredictable. They planned to know the route like the back of their mittens...just in case.

Chapter Four

She'd had to wait twenty-four days, three hours and twenty-seven minutes, but finally it was time to race! The airplane ride from Yellowknife to Norman Wells had been exciting, but not nearly as exciting as what was coming next.

"Here you go, Jaz," Liz, the dogs' owner, said, holding a panting, squirming sled dog by the collar. He was black with white tufts on his chest and tail, short-haired compared to most of the dogs in the kennel. "As you can see, Scooby's all ready for you!" Scooby was hopping on his two back legs as if to say, "Let's go! Let's go!" Just like the other dogs, he was wearing fuzzy felt booties, designed to keep his feet warm and protected from ice cuts.

Liz and Nick Poitras were the owners of Mountain Dream Vacations, a company that led tours of the

Mackenzie River and the historic Canol Trail—by canoe, with sled dogs and on foot. They had agreed to share their dog teams with the JCRs. Two other adventure outfitters in the area had done the same.

Destiny Patrol, along with the JCR patrols from nine other communities in the Northwest Territories, had descended on Norman Wells for two days of racing with their assigned five-dog teams. The teams were shared, and the races staggered.

On day one, the first set of teams had taken off, and Jaz had cheered them on. On day three, the next group had raced, and Jaz had cheered again. Finally it was day five, and Jaz was through with cheering. She grabbed hold of Scooby's collar and walk-danced him over to where Colly was waiting patiently.

"Hurry up, Jaz, bring him over!" Colly said.

Okay, not so patiently. "Hold your puppies, Colly, I'm coming."

"That's not how the saying goes."

"It is now!"

There were JCRs, rangers and volunteers almost everywhere she looked. It seemed like the whole town of Norman Wells was involved in billeting and feeding JCRs. It felt like a big exciting summer fair, except, of course, it wasn't summer.

Mid-March in Norman Wells meant the rivers were still frozen solid, even though there was a kiss of sunshine in the air, the promise of spring. It was a perfect time and a beautiful place to race.

From Liz and Nick's place, Jaz could see the Franklin Mountain Range to the east, the Mackenzie Mountain Range to the west, and the great wide Mackenzie River in the middle, making its way north to the Arctic Ocean.

"Come on, Jaz…today?"

"Fine, let's go!"

She clicked Scooby onto their lead line and was rewarded with a sloppy lick across the face. While she settled into the belly of their sled, Colly pushed off from the back.

"Hike! Hike! Gee!" Colly called, telling the team to get moving and turn to the right.

The staging area on the surface of the Mackenzie River was chaotic. Dogs yipped and crooned; wood smoke and onion smells filled the air. Somewhere, someone was playing a fiddle while JCRs laughed and gobbled hot dogs prepared by smiling cooks hovering over huge barbecues. All the JCRs wore white bibs with black numbers. The green hoods of their Junior Ranger sweatshirts were either pulled over their heads or rested on their backs. Above the numbers, the names of their patrols had been painted in. Spotting the distinct gold-tinted red lettering of Destiny Patrol, Jaz waved at George and Shelby.

Two sharp blasts of a whistle quieted the laughter. The dogs, somehow knowing it was time to hush, settled in their spots, ears forward, panting.

"Welcome, JCRs!" a ranger leader called out, his voice magnified through a bullhorn.

It was Major Chris—Jaz could tell by his French accent. Major Chris was one of the people who had started the whole Junior Ranger program in the late 1990s. Whenever he could, he took a break from his office headquarters in Yellowknife to help with the big events.

"JCRs," he said, "you have been preparing for months, and I want to congratulate each of you for making it here. I also want to go over a few points before we start the race."

A roaring cheer interrupted Major Chris. He lowered the bullhorn and clapped along with everyone else until it was quiet again.

"We will send you out one team at a time, at two-minute intervals, which we will keep track of and subtract from your total time at the end of each day," he said. "If you want to pass another team, what do you say?"

"On by!" Jaz shouted, along with everyone else.

"Okay, I didn't quite hear that, but if you said 'Pizza pie,' you'd better go get something more to eat. If you said 'On by,' you are correct."

He paused while the JCRs laughed.

"If a team calls 'On by' to you, you must pull to the side of the trail and wait. If you do not, you will be asked to leave the race. At every checkpoint, you must have one of our rangers sign off on each task before you can proceed. Before you get to the tasks, you must feed your dogs. If you do not, you will be asked to leave the race. Will I need to ask any of you to leave the race?"

"No, sir!" was the united shout, this one clear.

"Good. Stay safe, stay with your partners, and have fun!"

Major Chris lowered his bullhorn and waited for the first team to reach the start line before he raised his starter pistol.

It was time to race! Their entire route would cover only a tiny part of the Canol Trail. Each team would begin by crossing the Mackenzie River. From there, they would head across the flatlands and then enter the Mackenzie Mountain Range through Dodo Canyon.

There would be three checkpoints, and at each they would stop and test their skills. At Checkpoint Three, the end of Dodo Canyon, they would turn around and make their way back to the beginning. If the dogs ran at average speeds, the race should take about six hours each way. No matter how fast they went, they weren't allowed to run their teams for more than six hours. Overnight camps were set up at Checkpoints Two and Three.

One by one, teams set off amid cheers. By the time Jaz reached the start line with Colly, her voice was already hoarse.

Major Chris raised his starter pistol. *Crack!*

They were off at last!

"Hike! Hike!" Colly shouted, while Jaz made kissy sounds to encourage the dogs to run faster. She leaned forward in the sled, feeling every fold and bump on the river through her bent knees despite the blanket and her thick fleece pants. She and Colly had drawn straws to see who would drive the team first. Jaz couldn't wait for her turn behind the sled.

Their team was fast! Scooby, their lead dog, was a wiry black ball of born-to-run, even if he didn't look much like a typical sled dog. Behind Scooby were Copper, Lady, Paws and Boone, all Mackenzie River huskies with long legs, creamy faces and coats glinting silver, gold and copper in the sun.

The weather forecast was for a mix of sun and cloud over the next few days, with occasional snow flurries—typical March weather. Right now, the sun was smiling. It felt good. Jaz hoped it would hold.

The Mackenzie River was five miles wide. On the other side lay Camp Canol. At the Norman Wells Museum, Jaz had learned that during World War II it had been a bustling town, built in haste as a pipeline was laid through the mountains. Back then Camp Canol had a hospital, a store, a church, army barracks and a dance hall. Now it was a ghost town, mostly demolished in the 1970s.

They raced silently through deserted streets, hearing only the sound of the sled over snow and the panted *ha, ha, ha* of the dogs.

"On by!" Colly called out as they overtook the team ahead of them.

Fort Resolution Patrol. Jaz could see their bibs as they pulled to the side.

"We'll get you later, you wait and see!" the boy on the back of the sled shouted. He was shaking his fist, but he was grinning too.

It felt good to be out on the trail. It was easy to

forget this was a race, and that only a few of them would get to go to Ottawa. Jaz wasn't forgetting, though. No way!

They had agreed in advance that they would change positions at each checkpoint so that they didn't have to stop along the way and lose precious minutes. Over the glassy ice of Heart Lake they passed a second team, and as they pulled up to Checkpoint One at Ray Creek, Jaz was excited to see they had just about caught up with a third team.

"Easy," Colly called to the dogs. "Whoa!" He staggered from the back of the sled while Jaz raced to a ranger with a clipboard. After she checked in, she scooped up a big bucket of food for the dogs.

Their first skills test was in fire starting. When she returned from feeding the dogs, Colly was already trying to light willow twigs with a match. They were given three matches per team. If they couldn't start a fire in three tries, they would have to take a time penalty and try again.

"Come on...come on, Colly," Jaz whispered, looking over his shoulder.

The first match flared.

And went out.

"You can do it, Colly."

Colly said nothing. He rubbed his hands and flexed his fingers. After shaking them out, he took another match.

Hiss!

It was lit! Carefully, hand shaking, he held it to the twigs.

Pffft.

It went out.

"Come *on*, Colly. Just one more chance!"

"Don't you think I know that?" he snapped.

His anger must have gotten the blood flowing through his hands, as they were no longer shaking. Jaz shifted her position to try and shield him from the breeze.

That did it. The flame caught and held.

It was Jaz's turn next. Easy-peasy. She would mix up the bannock, which they would cook over the fire, and they'd be on their way.

Flour in a pot.

Oil in the flour.

A pinch of salt.

Enough water to squish and knead.

Squish and knead, squish and knead. She was pretty good at this! Maybe she would make some for her dad. Maybe she would even make a special Dad 'n' Jazy Green Marshmallow Bannock.

"Jaz, that's good enough," Colly said, shoving a stick in front of her.

She wrapped half of the dough around it and passed it back to Colly, taking time to make a face at him. She wrapped the rest of the dough on another stick, which she kept. Together they turned their sticks this way and that over the flame until their bannock was golden brown.

"Ready!" Colly shouted.

The ranger with the clipboard broke off a piece, nibbled and nodded.

"You're good to go," he said.

Stuffing one hunk of the bannock in her mouth and the rest in her coat pocket for later, she ran with Colly back to their waiting team.

"Hike!" she called. Scooby responded with a gleeful bark and hunkered back onto the trail.

Soon the trail narrowed so much that, if she had wanted to, she could have reached out and slapped the tips of willow shoots as if they were the hands of an eager crowd at the finish line. Except for the sounds of the sled and dogs, it was serene. It was a time to recharge and breathe in the colors; the sky was as blue as a painted ocean on a globe. The scrub lining the trail was a collage of winter gold, brown and green.

Green.

"Whoa!" she called.

"What are you doing, Jaz? Why are you stopping?"

"I see something," she said, stepping off the back of the sled.

"Are you nuts?" Colly shouted. "We have a plan, and stopping to sightsee isn't part of the plan!"

Jaz ignored him, reached into the brush and pulled out...a hat.

A green flat-cap.

"This is Gunther's," she said.

Chapter Five

"It's not Gunther's. Get back on the sled!" Colly bellowed. He glanced behind them to see if anyone was catching up.

Stuffing the hat in her pocket, Jaz looked behind her too. No one was coming. Yet.

She gave her head a shake. What was she thinking? Of course it wasn't Gunther's. They were way too far from Yellowknife, and why would he come here, anyway?

She jumped back on the sled. "Hike, hike!"

But what if it was Gunther's hat?

Stranger things had happened. After all, if pet cats can save people from burning buildings, and kids can fly airplanes, why couldn't Gunther be hiking along the Canol Trail?

Because it was winter. No one hiked the Canol Trail in winter.

Scooby and his team leapt ahead again, as if they had never stopped. Their tongues were lolling out of their open mouths, and their tails were high. Jaz knew by watching them that for these dogs there was nothing in the world better than running.

Running.

"Colly, what if Gunther is on the run and taking the Canol Trail to the Yukon?"

Colly craned his head around so he could look at her. "Why would Gunther be on the run, and why would he end up here? Were you born insane or was it something you ate?"

Jaz gripped the sled more tightly, fighting an impulse to bop him on top of the head. "Rude!" she cried, the word exploding from her belly like a firecracker.

"Sorry, Jaz, but why would Gunther come all the way up here without telling anyone?"

She frowned. "I know it sounds crazy, but maybe someone is chasing him. Maybe they're after top secret diamond-polishing information, and maybe that's why the Diamond Squad is involved!"

"Jaz..."

"Colly, I'm sure this is Gunther's hat. I've never seen another one like it, ever."

"It's just a stupid hat. There's got to be lots of them around. You just haven't been looking."

"This is a summer hat, but Gunther wears it winter and summer, and he's had it for as long as I can remember."

Colly hesitated and then shook his head. "It can't be his. Some hiker must have dropped it last summer. "

"Nope. If they did, it would have been under the snow all winter. It would be gross by now. This isn't gross."

She shoved it over Colly's shoulder. He took it from her and turned it this way and that before tucking it in their pack.

"It's not Gunther's," he insisted, folding his arms. "Look, forget the hat and start thinking about the race!"

Jaz felt a growl build in her belly, but she let it go because they were coming up fast to the old white army tent with a bright orange roof that marked the emergency shelter right before the Carcajou River. Checkpoint Two was beside the emergency shelter. They'd run this leg of the trail in about an hour. If they kept their speed up, they would be well on their way to winning!

This time, roles reversed, Colly raced to sign in and get the dogs their snack, while Jaz wobbled off the back of the sled.

Uh-oh. A quick glance told Jaz that her test would be with air rifles. It wasn't that she didn't like shooting air rifles, but she hadn't been doing it long enough to get good at it. At least Colly wouldn't be looking over her shoulder. Dogs fed, he was sent to test his snare-making abilities. Double darn. She was pretty good at snares! Oh well, she would have a chance at that test during the return leg of the race. First she had to make it through this one.

Air rifle in hand, Jaz settled on her belly and peered at her goal. She had five shots to hit three of the targets or there would be a time penalty and she would have to try again—just like with the fire-starting test. Wiggling into the snow, trying to get comfortable, she pushed her sunglasses to the top of her head and peered through her rifle sight. The breeze had picked up a little, causing small puffs of ice crystals to whiff against her cheeks and eyes. She blinked them away, feeling sun-tears freeze to her lashes.

No good. Her eyes were blurry.

She lowered the rifle and ripped off her gloves to

wipe the moisture from her eyes. Vision clear again, she put her sunglasses back on and took aim, trying to remember what she'd been taught. She ran down a mental checklist. Butt plate snug against her shoulder. Check. Body position flat, not twisted; right knee forward. Check.

A commotion behind her told her another team had arrived at the checkpoint. Butterflies began beating against the sides of her belly. Everything in her screamed HURRY! But she knew she had to take her time. A hurried shot would be a wasted shot.

"Hurry up, Jaz!" Colly shouted, coming up behind her, obviously finished with his own task. "It's George and Shelby."

Great! Next to Colly, George was the very best shot in Destiny Patrol. There was no way she could outshoot him. She tried to block out everything but her rifle, her body position and the target.

A body slammed into the snow beside her. It was Shelby—thank goodness! Shelby was good, but not as good as George. There was still a chance Jaz and Colly could pull out ahead.

"Jaz, it isn't rocket science. Would you just shoot!" Colly cried. Jaz imagined slapping a big piece of duct tape over his mouth.

Shelby had made her first shot. Jaz couldn't tell whether it had been a hit or a miss.

She peered down the sight, took aim and...

Dang! She'd forgotten to take off the safety.

"Jaz, for crying out..." Colly swallowed the rest of his complaint.

Another shot from Shelby.

Okay, okay. She could still do this. Body straight, knee bent, holding stock, aim...*PING*!

It was a hit!

Shelby had just gotten off her third shot. All she needed was three out of the five shots to move on. Nope. She was aiming again. They were still okay.

Jaz lined up again, trying not to hear Colly's not-so-subtle sounds of impatience. Heavy sigh. Heavier sigh. He was starting to sound like a big old windbag, which was about right, anyway.

Body straight, knee bent, holding stock, aim... *THHPP*! Dang! This time it was a miss.

Another shot from Shelby. That was four, and she was still lining up. Maybe she was hurrying too much.

Carefully, Jaz lined up again. *PING*! Hit! She needed one more and had two shots left. If she missed those, she would take a time penalty.

Shelby had just fired her fifth shot and was on her feet, dashing toward the watching ranger.

"I need more ammo!" Shelby called.

That meant Jaz still had a chance.

Body straight, knee bent, aim...*PING*! It was good!

"Yeah!" Colly cheered and clapped her on the back.

George whacked her hand in a high five as they dashed past. "Yeah, good going, but just wait until the way back!"

Scooby bugled his hello as they ran toward him, and the team leapt to its feet, ready to run. Jaz settled into the belly of the sled, and Colly hopped on the back to drive.

The next portion of the trail would be a bit tricky and was the longest, slowest leg of the race. It should take two hours to get to the next checkpoint, which was the halfway mark, but they hoped to do it in less.

Unlike the Mackenzie River, which was wide and pretty straight near Norman Wells, the Carcajou was twisty, with open fast-running water in some places and covered with deep soft snow, in others. The Carcajou was a test in itself to see how well the JCRS were able to follow the marked trail. If they strayed from the path, they would end up either in water or waist-deep snow.

Jaz climbed out of the sled, and they both ran alongside, helping the dogs where they could with a push or a lift when the sled got jammed in the ice.

On the other side of the Carcajou, they could see where Dodo Canyon opened up as if to welcome them. Its walls, all sheer rock and snow, looked like the side of a cake with icing dripping down. Inside the canyon, the trail was wide and smooth except in places where the river had kicked up curls of frozen ice. The dogs steadied their pace, and again Jaz was lulled by the gentle *ha, ha, ha* of their breathing.

The open stretches felt like a gimme—relaxation time. With the sun's warmth and the easier pace, Jaz almost forgot they were racing.

"Colly?" she asked, yawning.

"Yeah, Jaz."

"Why are your eyes blue?"

"What's the big deal about my eyes?"

"Nothing, I guess, but I want to know why you won't tell me."

She waited.

"Look, it's not such a big deal, Jaz. I was just bugged because you never shut up—no offense."

"None taken."

She waited again.

"Are you going to tell me?"

"Fine! It's just a family thing, Jaz."

Facing forward, she couldn't see him, but she could hear the impatience in his voice. "But I thought you were Dene. Dene have brown eyes."

"Not all Dene, Jaz. Not in my family, anyway."

This was like pulling teeth! "Who else in your family has blue eyes, Colly?"

When he didn't answer right away, she wondered if he'd decided to ignore her. Finally he spoke.

"My grandfather had blue eyes, and so did his grandfather. They say it usually skips a generation, and it goes as far back as anyone can remember."

"That's cool! I don't know why you didn't want to tell me."

"Look, I'm proud of my heritage, Jaz. It's just that my eyes got me beat up when I was younger. Kids pushed me around."

Jaz didn't know what to say to that. She knew kids got bullied sometimes, but she had never been on the receiving end of it.

"So what happened when they pushed you around?"

"When I got big enough, I pushed back."

Jaz closed her eyes in the sunshine, trying to imagine what it must be like to be a blue-eyed Dene boy with a blue-eyed grandfather and great-great-grandfather. That was really special. Maybe he was bullied because the others were jealous. More likely he was bullied because he was different. Maybe that was why he was so uptight all the time.

At Checkpoint Three, teams were given the option of halting for the night or, if they were in soon enough, carrying on back to Checkpoint Two. Jaz and Colly were in early and expected Shelby and George would be close behind. There was no question—they were carrying on.

After working together on a drill involving setting up a tent, they were back on the sled. Jaz pedaled her right foot against the trail, trying to help the dogs pick up extra speed. Clouds had tiptoed over the canyon, muting the brightness of the day.

"Still no sign of Shelby and George," Colly said, twisting around to face her. "But they could catch us on the way back. If I end up shooting against George, we could be in trouble."

"You'll be fine, Colly. I know it!" Jaz was surprised at how much she wanted to encourage him.

Colly smiled and his face lit up in a way Jaz hadn't seen before.

The sudden wind also surprised her. Unlike the brief gusts that had kicked up soft snow earlier in the race, this wind felt like it was winding around and around, swooshing up one side of the canyon wall and then down the other. Blindly, Jaz grasped the sled as ice crystals, like a flurry of tiny diamonds, stung her face. They slipped behind her sunglasses, forcing her eyes shut. She pushed one gloved hand to her eyes, knocking the sunglasses into the sled. Just as well. They were useless in this swirling wind.

"To the side!" Colly shouted. "Follow the canyon wall!"

The dogs might be able to find their way, but they couldn't take a chance. They were going fast enough that if they hit something, they could do real damage. Using the left side of the canyon as a guide, they advanced slowly.

As suddenly as the snow squall had come upon them, it was gone.

"Whoa!" Jaz cried, as much to herself as to stop the dogs.

Dodo Canyon was wide. This one was not.

They'd entered a chasm, but that wasn't what tied

her tongue. Farther in she could see a snowmobile, half hidden and upside down behind a jagged boulder. Jaz urged the dogs forward. This time, Colly didn't protest.

Beside the snowmobile, something had stained the snow red. Blood?

Colly leapt from the sled and ran toward the overturned machine. Jaz halted the dogs and followed him.

Because of all the map work she and Colly had done, Jaz knew they were in Echo Canyon, a narrow offshoot of Dodo Canyon with towering walls and no way out.

"Where'd they go?" Jaz asked, looking around her. The machine had been abandoned.

"I'm more concerned about this blood. Look!"

Snow from the squall had only partly covered what looked like a trail made by someone trying to drag themselves away. Peeking out from behind a boulder was a boot. She and Colly dashed toward it. Sure enough, attached to the boot was a man.

The man was holding a rifle, and it was pointed their way.

"Hello, Jaz," Gunther said.

Chapter Six

Jaz froze, for once too shocked to speak. Well, almost. "We found your hat," she squeaked.

"You're Gunther Wegener?" Colly asked.

"Yes," Gunther said, wincing. He shifted uncomfortably from his not-so-good hiding place behind the boulder. There was a gash on his head. Blood was matted into his sandy brown hair and smeared the side of his face.

"What are you doing here, Gunther...and what's with the gun?" Jaz asked. One side of her brain told her she should be afraid, but the other side said this was Gunther. Gunther was a nice man. She closed her eyes and opened them again, hoping that she was imagining him. She wasn't.

Gunther lowered the gun but didn't set it aside. It was clear that at any moment he might point it at them again. "I am sorry it has to be this way, Jaz, but I am going to need your help."

Colly must have been afraid Jaz would make a fuss, because he put his hand on her arm, as if to stop her. "Sure we'll help, but you don't need that gun."

Gunther looked relieved but continued gripping the gun. "Come here, Jaz."

Hesitantly, she took one step and then another. When she was close enough, he told her to stop.

"Get that sled ready," he said to Colly, his voice strained. "Clear a space inside for two, and put the packs from my snowmobile on it."

He pulled himself upright, leaning awkwardly against the boulder. "Just be good, Jaz, and I will not have to use this gun."

"But why, Gunther?" Jaz cried. "I don't understand."

"Sometimes things happen. I cannot explain to you."

Jaz's head was whirling. Had Gunther done something bad after all? Were the police after him? It was all too confusing.

"Here is what we will do," Gunther said as Colly returned. "It will be dark soon. As soon as it is, we will continue through Dodo Canyon toward Blue Mountain."

"But Norman Wells is the other way."

"I know that, Jaz."

Jaz thought a moment, processing what he had said. Gunther wasn't looking to get to a hospital. He was going to keep running, and he was going to take them with him. "You must know you're trapped," she said, ignoring Colly's warning glare.

"Yes, I know. That is how I ended up here, smashing my snowmobile." He cursed under his breath. At least, Jaz thought it was a curse. She wasn't sure, because it was in German.

"People are expecting us!" she cried.

"Then we will go quickly," he said. His skin looked gray beneath his whiskers. Gunther never used to have whiskers. "As soon as it is dark."

Jaz and Colly exchanged glances. Despite what she'd said, there was a chance they might not be missed, at least not right away. Checkpoint Three had marked that they were on their way back to Checkpoint Two, but Checkpoint Two wouldn't know that. They might not figure it out until everyone stopped for the night. They weren't exactly in a position where they could set off their emergency flares. They stood still for what felt like a very long time. After a while, when Gunther nodded okay, they sat. Jaz could feel the cold seeping into her limbs in a way it never did when she was moving. It was getting colder. Her bum went numb and she stood again, stamping her feet. Gunther kept close watch, saying nothing.

In the crevasse all was still, but Jaz noticed wisps of low cloud whipping over the sliver of sky. She knew it meant that beyond their sheltered waiting space, the wind had picked up again. Except for the wind, it was quiet. So close to nightfall, they must have been one of the last teams allowed to pass.

Jaz didn't actually see the sun set, but the sky darkened, and then it was night. Night still came early at this time of year. Jaz figured it was just past 7:00.

"Okay, now we go," Gunther said.

He motioned Jaz into the sled first and then he limped over to it in obvious pain. He sat facing her and Colly, his back to the dogs. "You will drive," he said to Colly. "I don't need to tell you to be good."

The reality of their situation sank into Jaz like a stone. Gunther had a gun. Gunther was taking them hostage—just like in the movies, only this was for real. She began to sniffle.

"I must do this, Jaz," Gunther said. He was looking at her, but his eyes seemed to go somewhere else. "I am sorry."

"Please, Gunther...you're hurt. Maybe things aren't as bad as you think." She was trying not to cry but couldn't stop a few sneak-away tears. She swiped at her eyes to stop her lashes from freezing together. Whatever happened, she needed to keep her eyes open!

"Do as you are told, and I won't shoot you. Make no mistake, though," he added, his voice hard. "I will shoot you if you make noise or do anything I don't tell you to do. Now let us go—quietly!"

Quiet didn't matter much once they turned back into Dodo Canyon. In the open space, wind had whipped up soft snow, just as it had before they'd taken their wrong turn. It beat against her cheeks and filled her ears with a hollow whistle, like the sound of blowing over the top of a bottle. The moon was a fingernail playing peekaboo behind fast-moving clouds, making the snow glow just enough to light their way. This time they followed the right side of the canyon. Through the dark and the snow, Jaz could see light from the shelter at Checkpoint Three, where the canyon opened up. As they passed, a dog howled, then another and another.

The dogs knew they were there! They would be rescued!

As soon as she thought that, ice settled into her belly. If people came running out, Gunther might decide to shoot. She'd never seen Gunther like this, but she had seen movies. In the movies, the bad guys always shoot first.

It didn't seem possible, but Gunther had become a bad guy. Why? How?

No one came running out—not that she could tell, anyway. Stupid snow! As they passed, she could hear singing coming from one of the white tents, bright in the moonlight.

As they left Dodo Canyon and began climbing the sloping trail beyond, Jaz heard hope whisper good-bye.

Chapter Seven

After about an hour of travel, cramped in the sled's belly, knees bent, facing Gunther, Jaz's toes began to tingle with pins and needles. Wiggling them only made it worse. At least the wind had settled, except for the occasional gust. She imagined that behind the sled they were leaving a clear trail in the moonlight. Unfortunately, because of the earlier flurries, it might take some time for searchers to find it.

Except for once or twice when his head nodded briefly toward his chest, Gunther hadn't looked away from her. He held on to his gun as if his hands were frozen in place. His face looked gaunt in the shadows against the night-glow of snow. He didn't look like Gunther at all.

And he wasn't. Not the Gunther she knew.

They passed some of the infamous Canol Trail "junk." An old yellow truck from the 1940s sat half-buried in snow, long since stripped of anything of value, its windows broken. Its hood had partly caved into the space where an engine should be.

"Gunther, please tell us where we're going," she pleaded. "What's after Blue Mountain?"

"Russia," he answered.

She wasn't sure she'd heard right; Colly said nothing. Actually, except for calling cues to the dogs, Colly had said nothing since they'd begun this insane trek. That worried her. Colly quiet might mean Colly planning. She hoped he wasn't planning anything stupid.

"You didn't need to do this, Gunther. We would have helped you."

He shook his head. "You are a good person, Jaz, and I am sure your friend is too."

"Colly," Jaz said. "My friend's name is Colly. You're a good person too, Gunther. Why are you kidnapping us?"

Gunther made a sound like choking. "I am sorry, Jaz, but sometimes things happen that we never expect. Bad things."

She heard sniffling and stared hard, trying to see Gunther's face. "Gunther...are you okay?"

He snorted, took one hand off his gun and wiped his face.

"Whoa," Colly called, and the dog team slowed to a stop. Beside the trail were what looked like two old train cabooses stuck in the snow, with a smashed-in trailer just behind. More Canol junk.

"I did not tell you to stop," Gunther said.

"I don't know where we're going," Colly said. "You said Russia. We can't get to Russia from here. That doesn't make sense."

Jaz looked over her shoulder. Colly was standing up straight and stiff on the sled, as if he had a board up the inside of his parka. He looked cold and angry.

"We will be met," Gunther said.

"Where?" Colly snapped. It sounded as if there was more he wanted to say but was holding himself back. Barely.

"Take it easy, Colly," Jaz said. She looked back and forth between Gunther and Colly, her stomach tightening.

Despite the bite of cold and fear, this didn't feel real. What had happened to the nice man who smiled and gave her strudel? If she could only get him to talk, maybe they could find a way out of this. Maybe whatever had happened could be fixed. She had to give it a shot.

"Gunther, you said that sometimes bad things happen. Did something bad happen to you? Are you running away?"

Gunther rubbed his forehead. Somewhere in the distance, Jaz heard a wolf howl, and then another. She shivered, and not because of the cold.

"No, Jaz. Nothing happened to me. It is something far worse."

"What?"

"You do not need to know. You need only to listen and do what I tell you to do."

"Most people say I'm not very good at listening or doing as I'm told."

Was that a smile? Hard to tell in the dark.

"Look, we're in the middle of the mountains, and it's not like we're going anywhere else. Please, Gunther...I'm scared. If you tell me what happened, maybe at least I can understand why we are here."

He didn't move for a long while, and Jaz wondered if he'd even heard her.

"Okay, but not here," he said finally. "I will tell you as we travel."

If Colly was satisfied with Gunther's answer, he didn't say, but he did start up the team again. "Hike!"

Despite his promise, Gunther didn't say anything. He seemed preoccupied and leaned from one side of the sled to the other, his head nodding and jerking up again, like a weight on a fishing line. She would just have to get him started.

"You said something very bad happened, but that it didn't happen to you. What was it, Gunther?"

His shoulders slumped. "My family," he said, his voice catching. "They should never have left Germany."

Jaz frowned. She knew Gunther had grown up in Germany, but she didn't know anything about his family. He'd never spoken of them when she popped by the café, and they had never come to visit. Not that she knew of, anyway. She waited for him to continue.

"A long time ago, I had a friend. We grew up together. He was a good boy—I was a good boy—but sometimes we got into a bit of trouble." He stopped and took a deep breath. "He got into more trouble, and after a while I did not see him anymore."

He paused. For a long time he didn't speak.

"Then what happened?" Jaz asked, hoping he was still awake.

Gunther cleared his throat and coughed. "When I wanted to come to Canada, I had some trouble because of some of the things I did when I was young. Then I ran into my old friend, and he said he could help."

"Did he help?" she asked.

"Yes," he said, his voice bitter. "He made things right with my application. He said he had friends. When I asked how I could thank him, he told me not to worry about it. He said maybe someday he would need a favor."

"Haw," Colly called, not too loudly, as if not wanting to interrupt. "Haw!"

Vaguely, Jaz was aware of the team turning.

"After my mother died, my sister and her boy, my little nephew Luka, wanted to leave Germany to be closer to me. He helped with that too."

"They came to Yellowknife?"

"No, not Yellowknife. There was a good job for my sister in Vancouver, so that is where they moved."

"Haw," Colly called.

"Where are you going?" Gunther asked. He didn't sound alarmed. Mostly he sounded tired.

"Just following the trail," Colly said. "It's tricky here. Haw!"

Colly was up to something, she was sure of it. She'd studied the maps just as much as Colly had, and she knew there were no bends like this. They were turning around!

"What was the favor, Gunther?" Jaz asked in a rush. Maybe she could distract him. "What did your friend want?"

"Haw!" Colly called again.

"What are you doing?" Gunther shouted. "You stop—now!"

"Whoa!" Colly cried. He sounded frightened.

"I know what you are doing. Get us back on track, NOW!"

Dumb-noodle! she shouted in her head. Fear landed in a lump in her belly, making her want to throw up, but she wasn't sure if it was because Colly had been caught or because he'd tried in the first place.

"Gee!" Colly called to the dogs, his voice tight. "Gee! Gee!"

"Wait a minute," Gunther said after they had returned to the trail. As the team slowed to a stop, he pulled their red emergency supply bag onto his knees and opened it.

"It is obvious that I cannot trust you." He rummaged through the pack, found their emergency flares and tossed them into the brush.

Jaz bit her lip. Whatever ground she had gained by getting Gunther to open up was lost, thanks to Colly. Didn't he notice that Gunther was softening? Why couldn't he just trust her to handle it? Because he was a control freak, that was why!

They carried on in the dark, not speaking. Only the wind and the sound of the sled swooshing over fresh snow broke the silence.

"Whoa!" Colly called.

Jaz could hear open water.

That wasn't all she heard.

Woooooo!

Wolves. And they were close!

Chapter Eight

"We will be fine," Gunther said, swinging his gun in the direction of the howling.

"Maybe," Colly said. "But how are we going to get across the river?"

Jaz peered into the night, her heart thudding. The trees were thicker here and taller, blocking out much of the moonlight reflecting off the snow. She knew from the map that this must be the Little Keele River and that there was a shelter around here somewhere. That is, unless Colly had taken them off track.

Woooo! Woooo!

The wolves were joining in a chorus. What if they came after them? Her head said that wasn't likely. Wolves didn't chase people. But then again, they might smell Gunther's blood, and wolves did go after injured animals, no matter what kind they were.

"Colly, do you see the shelter anywhere?" she asked. "We could go there."

"No!" Gunther said. He spat over the side of the sled. "I cannot take the chance that someone is coming after you. We must go on. It is not much farther."

"What about the open water?" Colly asked.

"We will try upstream."

Scooby growled, low and soft, as the wolves howled again. Jaz shivered, but not from cold.

"Hike! Gee!" Colly called to the dogs.

Slowly, they traveled along the river's edge. Finally Colly stopped the team. "I think we can cross here," he announced.

"Good," Gunther said, not looking.

"You should both get out of the sled, just in case."

"No," Gunther said, still not looking.

"But we don't know the condition of the ice. What if it isn't safe?"

"None of this is safe. We are not getting out, and you will get us across. Now!"

"Fine," Colly mumbled. He moved back to the side of the sled, holding the handle, but not climbing on. "Hike!"

Jaz held her breath as they started to cross. Before

long they were jammed in soft snow. At least it wasn't water.

"It would be easier if you got out," Colly grumbled.

"No," Gunther said.

"Fine," Colly said again as he rocked the sled back and forth, with the dogs straining to help. Before long they were free.

Woooo!

That was close   much closer than before! The dogs stopped. They were all growling now, sniffing the air.

"I don't like this, Colly!"

"I don't like this either, Jaz. Hike! Hike!" He jumped back on the sled, and the dogs leapt forward.

Sploosh! They were in the water and through it again before Jaz had time to think about it. One hard bump of the sled against snow threw them forward. Gunther grunted—Jaz couldn't tell if it was from pain or surprise—and the sled steadied and carried on. With one final bump, they were across the river.

Wooooo! Woooo!

"Get back to the trail," Gunther gasped.

"Gee! Gee! Hike!" Colly shouted.

Jaz strained to see into the shadows. She was comforted by the dogs. They were running hard, pushed faster by Colly's calls and by her kissy sounds of encouragement. Surely if the wolves were too close, the dogs would freak.

Beyond the Little Keele River the trail smoothed and became hard and flat. The trees thinned as they climbed, and, thankfully, there were no running wolf shapes among them.

"Canol Lake is just ahead!" Colly announced. "There's a shelter there."

"Not that one," Gunther said. "Take the side trail to the left."

"What about the wolves?" Jaz cried. "We need shelter!"

"No, I know another place."

Jaz felt like crying, but Colly eased left as he was told.

The trail dipped lower here, and brush thickened on either side. Once again, cloud moved across the sky, making it even more difficult to see. Jaz gripped the sides of the sled while turning her head this way and that, watching for shapes, listening for anything that might be giving chase.

Again the sled jammed in snow, and Jaz was thrown forward. She noticed that Gunther moved the gun before it could jab into her.

Jaz breathed a small sigh of relief. Gunther had moved the gun. That meant he really didn't want to hurt her. Whatever had brought him to this, somewhere inside there was still a good man.

The dogs started growling, causing the hairs on the back of her neck to stand at attention.

"Hike!" Colly cried, urging the dogs forward. "How much farther, Gunther?"

"We should be there," Gunther mumbled.

"What?"

"He said we should be there," Jaz said, louder.

It was tough going in the soft snow. Colly couldn't get out and help the dogs, because if he did he would sink and fall behind. The dogs were able to travel lightly, but the sled didn't always cooperate.

"There!" Jaz shouted, pointing.

They'd reached a clearing. On the far side there was a small shack. As they drew closer, Jaz's heart sank. One wall of the shack was smashed in and half collapsed.

"It'll have to do," Colly said as Gunther dragged himself from the sled, clutching his pack tightly, and moved toward what was left of the shelter. He didn't seem to care if they were coming or not. From the darkness there came a low woofing sound—almost a bark, but not quite. It was followed by another. Again the dogs growled.

This time she could see shadowy wolf shapes moving from the brush into the clearing.

"They've found us!" Jaz cried.

Chapter Nine

For a minute, no one moved. Slowly, Gunther raised his rifle and then lowered it. "I cannot see well enough," he muttered.

"Just shoot in the air!" Jaz whispered, though she didn't know why she was whispering. Her blood was snap-crackling through her veins while her mind and body were screaming *run*! But there was nowhere to run to.

Again he raised his rifle, aiming it above the tree-tops. *Crack*!

The dark shapes bounded away and melted into the night.

They waited for them to return, listening to the wind. The dogs settled into the snow, unconcerned. If the wolves were still there, they were keeping their distance.

"We need to start a fire," Colly said and began gathering what he could find, careful not to stray far from the shelter. He motioned Jaz near and whispered, "We can go now, while your friend is checking out the shed."

"Are you crazy? He still has a gun."

"Maybe we can get the gun away from him."

"Colly, I get it that you don't like to be pushed around, but a man with a gun, even if he is someone I know, is much more dangerous than your typical bully."

In the night, Colly's eyes didn't look blue anymore. They looked dark and angry. "This isn't about being bullied, Jaz. It's about staying alive!"

"Trying to grab the gun away from Gunther isn't the best way to stay alive."

Colly looked like he wanted to scream. She watched him take a deep breath.

"Why do you always have to argue, Jaz? Are you like this with everyone, or just me?"

She opened her mouth and then shut it again. Maybe there was just something about Colly that got her back up, or maybe she'd picked up the habit from her mom and dad. More than anything, she wanted to tell him this was all his fault; if he hadn't tried that little trick on the trail, maybe they *could* have made a run for it. Nope, thanks to Colly, Gunther didn't trust them. He was probably watching them from the shed.

She wanted to tell him all of that and more, but she kept her mouth shut. Arguing wasn't going to help anything.

Another howl in the distance made Jaz grab for Colly's arm and hold tight. "Just don't do anything stupid…please? We're a long way from finding help."

He shook her away and dumped the wood he'd gathered in front of the shed. "Come on. Here's your chance to prove you're better at starting a fire than me, Miss Perfect."

He moved a few feet away and sat down hard on the snow.

Stupid Colly. This was no time to have a temper tantrum.

As much as she hated to admit it, Colly was right about them having to do *something*. They were far away from help, and getting farther. If Gunther wouldn't let them go, they had to escape before they ended up in Russia or wherever it was that he was taking them.

Jaz sat down beside Colly and leaned close to his ear. "Okay, maybe we do have to get away," she whispered. "I just don't think this is a good time."

Colly glanced in the direction of the shed, then back at her. "When?"

She thought. "He is hurt pretty bad. I'll try talking to him again. Maybe if he relaxes enough he'll go to sleep. We can sneak away then."

"Fine. But if that doesn't work…"

"It'll work." She wished she felt as sure as she sounded.

She left Colly to start the fire and ducked into the shelter. Gunther was slumped over his pack as if he wanted to get something out of it but lacked the strength.

"Can I help you find something, Gunther?"

"Yes, Jaz. I have candles and matches in here. Get them for me, please."

Inside Gunther's pack she found three fat white candles wrapped in tissue paper, along with a small metal canister with matches in it. She lit one of the candles and set all three on a ledge running along the inside of the shed's wall. Lighting one candle at a time would help them last longer. It wasn't much light, but it was better than nothing.

"You're bleeding, Gunther."

"I know that, Jaz."

The whole side of his head was dark and sticky

looking. Blood had soaked into his coat and shirt, it looked as if he'd lost a lot of it. No wonder the wolves had found them.

He needed help.

Colly might call her crazy, and maybe he'd be right. Why would anyone want to help their kidnapper? The thing was, Gunther wasn't a kidnapper. Not by nature, anyway. Something very bad must have happened to make him so desperate.

If she left him, and he lost enough blood, he might pass out. Then she and Colly could get away.

But if he lost too much blood...he might die.

Gunther groaned and leaned against the side of the shed. She shook her head. No matter what, she couldn't leave him to bleed to death. "Gunther, we have peroxide and bandages in the sled. I can fix you up if you'll let me."

He nodded.

She retrieved their first-aid kit and began cleaning his wound. The fire blasted a measure of warmth through where there used to be a door. Colly joined them, bringing the dogs in with him. "We'll be warmer if we're all together," he said.

Jaz nodded and watched as the beasts, panting and happy, settled themselves in the corners of their cramped space. The air soon filled with the smells of camping and damp fur. The dogs were still attached to their towline. Maybe Colly thought it would be easier to move them quietly if they were in here with them. Made sense. If the dogs saw them sneaking out of the shed later, they might get excited, start howling and wake Gunther up. She turned back to her first-aid work as Colly watched, quietly stroking Scooby's head and neck.

When they'd found Gunther in Echo Canyon, he had been terrifying. Somehow, even with the gun, he didn't seem as bad anymore. Maybe it was because of his wound, or maybe it was because of what he had started to tell them back on the trail.

It was time to take a chance.

"Gunther?" she asked.

"What is it, Jaz?"

She dabbed carefully at his wound. "You wouldn't really shoot us, would you?"

He closed his eyes again as if he hadn't heard her. Finally, he spoke. "No, Jaz. I never could."

She let out a breath she didn't even know she'd been holding.

"Here, let me help," Colly said, taking a strip of gauze and placing it against Gunther's head. It didn't look like the bandage would help for long, but it was better than nothing. She sat back and let Colly take over.

"Gunther, you said your friend wanted you to do him a favor," she asked. "What was it?"

"At first it was nothing," Gunther said, his voice barely audible. Jaz had to strain to hear. "He was very helpful. He looked out for my mother, my sister and my sister's son. He became like family and was very good to my mother before she died. When he offered to move my sister and my nephew to Vancouver, I thought this was a good idea. We all did. Then one day he said that an associate had told him about the diamond company in Yellowknife. He suggested I apply for a job. He said it would be a good way to make a lot of money, which would help my sister. Moving would be expensive for her."

The diamond company... Jaz felt the buzz of a lightbulb beginning to flicker in her head.

"It sounds suspicious, Gunther."

"It is easy to say that now, Jaz, but I truly thought he was trying to help." He shook his head. "It was a difficult time."

She thought about the mixed-up paperwork in the news reports and what Colly had said when Gunther went missing. "Did your friend tell you to steal diamonds, Gunther?" She frowned. That didn't make sense. There were no diamonds missing.

"Not steal them, Jaz," he spat. "He gave me diamonds to take in. Terrible diamonds. Bad. He told me to make them into Canadian diamonds."

The lights in Jaz's head were all on now—a whole roomful of them!

"Did he give you blood diamonds, Gunther?"

He nodded.

"I know about blood diamonds from school! We were learning about human rights abuses and how in Africa…"

"Then you also know that Canadian diamonds are worth much more," he interrupted.

She nodded.

"All I had to do was etch the bad diamonds with the Canadian diamond mark. That was all," he said, his voice singsong, as if he'd said it to himself many times. "And then, of course, I had to get them out."

So that was why no diamonds had been reported missing. Gunther had taken the blood diamonds in and then taken them out again. They were never on the books. But there was still something she didn't get. "Why'd you go along with it, Gunther? No favor is worth doing something so wrong."

Gunther began weeping again, quietly, his eyes closed. Jaz saw Colly look toward the rifle. She poked him, shaking her head in answer to the question she read in his eyes. He lifted his hand as if to snatch the rifle anyway, but before he could do anything they might regret, Gunther opened his eyes again. "He said he would hurt him," Gunther said softly, tears welling. "This monster who said he was my friend."

"Hurt who, Gunther?" Jaz asked. She sat back and exchanged glances with Colly, waiting for Gunther to answer.

After sobbing quietly for a while, he took a deep breath and wiped at his face. "I am sorry. This is difficult." His face hardened. "They have taken Luka. This is why I have no choice."

Jaz felt ice rush through her veins. "They've kidnapped him?"

"Yes." Gunther began sniffling again. "He is only four years old!" he wailed.

Chapter Ten

Jaz glanced at Colly. He looked just as horrified as Jaz felt.

"You said 'they,'" Colly said. "Did your friend have help?"

"He is not my friend," Gunther spat. "He is with the Russian mob."

Jaz gulped. She didn't know much about the Russian mob, but if it was anything like the Italian Mafia, it was very, very bad.

"But if your nephew was kidnapped, why didn't we hear about it on the news?" Jaz asked.

"We could not report it. No police, they said. Or he will die." Gunther wiped his eyes. They were red and swollen. "Do you see? This is why I must give them what they want. When I do, they will give me my nephew."

She did see, and she could tell by the look on Colly's face that he understood too.

"Tomorrow we must go to the plateau on the south side of Blue Mountain. There will be a helicopter waiting, and I will give them their diamonds."

Colly nodded and frowned, resting his chin in his hands.

With nothing more to say, Gunther leaned his head back against the side of the shed and closed his eyes. It was all out in the open now. She understood that Gunther didn't feel he had a choice. A little boy was in grave danger.

Still, he had kidnapped them. Didn't that make him just as bad as the mob? Except the men in the mob would hurt little Luka if they didn't get their way. Gunther would never hurt Jaz and Colly, no matter what he had tried to make them believe.

She looked back at Gunther and saw his chest rising and falling evenly. He was sleeping. This time Colly made no move to take his gun. Outside, well beyond the crackling and popping of the fire, wolves howled. They sounded far away.

"What should we do?" Jaz whispered, not wanting to wake Gunther.

"What *can* we do, Jaz?" Colly whispered back.

"There must be something."

They sat for a long time, saying nothing. It was late

but Jaz felt no need to sleep. From time to time Colly fed the fire, or a dog would stir, but there was no more howling from the wolves. Perhaps the fire was keeping them away. That, and the threat of being shot.

"We need to go for help," Jaz said finally, her voice soft but determined.

Colly shook his head. "There's no way Gunther will make it up Blue Mountain on his own."

"That's why only one of us should leave," she said. "I have a plan."

"What is your plan?" Gunther asked.

She jumped. Gunther's eyes were open, though they lacked the desperation they'd held before. He just seemed tired. Resigned.

"Gunther, even if you give them the diamonds, they might go after your sister or grab Luka again. They might make you do this all over again."

"I am afraid of that," he admitted.

"Our only chance is to get you to the mountain while one of us goes back for help. You give them the diamonds, they'll give you Luka, and then the RCMP will catch them."

"You've been watching too many movies, Jaz," Colly said. "Things don't always work out that way in real life."

"They will this time. They have to!"

"Why don't we all just turn around right now? Gunther can explain everything to the RCMP, and then they can handle things on Blue Mountain."

"You know why. Because the Russians have to see Gunther and think everything is going as planned. Otherwise..." She gulped.

Gunther was nodding. "Yes, this is why I must bring the diamonds."

"But we also have to stop them, Gunther. Otherwise you and your family will never be safe."

"Yes," he said, so softly that Jaz could barely hear. "I know this too."

"Will you go along with the plan?"

They waited as Gunther closed his eyes, covering them with his hand. "Yes," he said finally. "It is what we must do."

"You know that even if you help the RCMP catch them, you'll probably still be in trouble," Colly said.

"I know this."

Now they only had to decide which one of them would stay with Gunther and which one would go for help.

No sweat.

Chapter Eleven

By dawn, in between restless catnaps and taking turns feeding the fire, they still had not agreed on who would go back for help and who would go up the mountain with Gunther.

"I'm not sending you up the mountain to meet the mob, Jaz," Colly said, rubbing his eyes. "But I can't let you go back on your own. You might get lost or be attacked by wolves."

"Let me?" she shouted, while Gunther held his head. "Who died and made you King Poop?"

"I outrank you."

"This isn't the patrol."

It rankled that Colly didn't think she was capable of doing the same things as him, but she tried not to let that get in the way of her thinking. Jaz pulled out the bannock she'd saved from the day before and shared it with Colly and Gunther. Scooby looked at her hopefully, and she broke off a taste of her piece for each of the dogs. Colly did the same. Gunther offered up all of his, saying he wasn't hungry.

They watched as Gunther got slowly to his feet. He gave a cry of pain as his knees gave way. He would have hit the ground if Colly hadn't caught him.

"That clinches it," Jaz said.

"What?"

"I'm not as big as you, and if Gunther fell on me I wouldn't be much help. You go with him, and I'll go back for help."

Colly cranked his neck to look Gunther in the face. "How long can we wait here, Gunther? When do you need to be at the mountain?"

"Noon."

"That's about five hours away. Jaz, there's no way you'll get all the way to Checkpoint Three by then, but maybe it won't matter. As long as we get Luka back, they can go after those guys anytime they want."

"I'd feel better if help came before the meeting," said Jaz.

"So would I, Jaz. Just stick to the trail and keep your eyes and ears peeled. There should be searchers out looking for us. Maybe you won't have to go all the way back."

Jaz nodded.

"One more thing…" He reached over and took the gun from Gunther, who did not resist. "Take this."

"But you'll need it! Those Russian guys will have guns…"

"And we won't have a chance against them. Don't worry. We won't do anything stupid."

She nodded. "There's one more thing. Gunther, I need you to write out what happened to you and what's supposed to happen now. I don't know if the RCMP will believe me otherwise, and we don't have much time."

While Gunther dug a pencil out of his pack and wrote on the back of one of their maps, Colly helped Jaz get ready for her trek. "Careful with this," Colly said, handing her the rifle. "It's a 30-30 with lever action. You already know a fair amount about rifle safety, but watch me again."

He went through the motions of removing the safety and showing her what she would need to do in order to shoot. Jaz was suddenly glad that Colly was best at everything in her JCR patrol.

"Thank you, Master Corporal," she said, grinning. He shot her a look.

"Remember, it's not an air rifle. If you do fire this thing, there'll be a kick."

"Wait," Gunther said as she readied to leave. He opened his pack and pulled out a small burlap package. Hands shaking, he untied it. Inside there were diamonds—maybe two hundred, maybe more. He handed her one. "Take this. It will help convince them."

She carefully placed the tiny gem, along with Gunther's confession, inside her zippered pocket.

Remembering the soft snow they'd encountered on their way in, Jaz set off on the first part of her trek wearing snowshoes. At first she hated how slow and chunky they made her feet feel, but after a time she felt the rhythm of them. *Huff-huff-huff*, she breathed gently. She'd always been pretty good at long-distance running at school, and she knew that even though she wanted to go faster, she shouldn't. Not if she wanted to make it all the way. Instead she concentrated on her body—breathe in, *tromp-tromp*, breathe out, *tromp-tromp*. She was so lost in her rhythm that she didn't notice the snow stinging her cheeks or the waving pine branches until she felt the need to wipe at her eyes and squeeze them to improve her vision.

"No, not another storm!" she shouted at the sky. She stopped. There was no sky. Not right now.

She panted, sweating inside her parka, wishing she'd remembered to bring her sunglasses. The snow was caking on her lashes. It was important to keep going. Moving forward again despite the blowing snow, she noticed their tracks from the night before were almost completely covered with snow. She wished it hadn't been dark when they were coming in. Was that her path straight ahead where the trees were thicker, or did it ease higher up the mountain where the way was less dense? Just what she needed—another choice!

The idea of making choices made her think of her mom and dad. "I wish you were here," she whispered tearfully, wiping her eyes. They couldn't help her run any faster, but at least she wouldn't feel so alone. Then again, if they were here they would only argue about what should be done and which way to go.

She shook her head. All she remembered seeing last night were the dark trees. Lots of trees. That was the way she would go.

The wind soon died down, and snow fell in great heavy flakes. She might have found it beautiful, except she knew that in thick snow there would be no airplanes flying, and even if there were, they wouldn't be able to see her. She gulped. If she got lost, there wouldn't be many tracks for a ground search to follow either.

After what felt like forever, the trees opened up a little, and she rejoined the main trail. She was exhausted and sweaty despite the chill. How long had she been running? It felt like maybe an hour…maybe more. So much farther to go.

She arrived at Little Keele River and, looking longingly at the small collection of shelters on the other side, wished she could stop, build a fire and sleep. She was cold, even though the temperatures were pretty mild. The bank on this side was steep, and she could hear open water. Still, it looked like she might be able to cross. Should she chance it? If she got wet, she might freeze to death.

Out of the corner of her right eye she saw movement. She turned and saw a velvet-nosed caribou gazing back at her. It shook its rich brown-and-cream coat and sniffed the air, as if trying to figure out what kind of an animal she was.

"Hello, girl," she said, deciding something so pretty, with such wet warm eyes, had to be a girl. You couldn't tell by the antlers. Jaz knew that both male and female caribou grow a new set of antlers each year.

Jaz watched as the beautiful beast veered to the left of the main trail and disappeared into scrubby trees.

She had an idea.

Breaking her promise to Colly, she left the trail and followed the caribou. Grunting, she pushed through the bush in what she hoped was the general direction of the river. The caribou must have noticed she was giving chase; it began to run. It was all she could do to keep its bobbing blond backside in sight.

Suddenly it was gone. She continued in the direction it had disappeared, and within moments she was skidding down the snow-covered riverbank.

She'd been right. The caribou knew the best place to get to the other side. She crossed the river in the caribou's tracks, and several minutes later she was back on the trail and running.

How long had it been? She was running like a machine. The snow stopped, then started again. Passing the same Canol junk they'd stopped at the night before, she hardly noticed it. Her legs were numb; she only knew they were pumping, pumping, pumping.

"Jaz!"

She fell headfirst into soft snow and didn't get up.

Chapter Twelve

"Holy-moley, Jaz, I can't believe we found you!"

"Actually, George, I think she found us," Shelby said. She wrapped a heavy blanket around Jaz while George peered at Jaz as if she'd grown two heads.

"I'm so glad to see you!" Jaz gasped, breathing hard, shaking the snow from her head. Her lungs ached, and now that she'd stopped she felt heavy, as if she had sunk into the ground and grown roots. More than anything, she wanted to curl into the blanket and sleep.

"Where's Colly?" Shelby asked, looking back down the trail from which Jaz had appeared.

Her relief vanished as quickly as it had come. "What time is it?"

"Ten thirty...No, wait. Ten thirty-seven. Where's Colly?" Shelby asked again. "Is he hurt?"

"No, but he could be if something goes wrong. We have to help him! Where's the RCMP?"

"The search master has us covering different areas with the rangers. Our team found some flares, and we thought they might be yours."

Jaz nodded.

"We found them off the main trail," Shelby continued. "The rest of our team is searching in that direction. We were assigned to wait at this spot and to call in every half hour on this." She pointed to the handheld radio. "We'd better call in."

While George talked into the radio, Jaz turned to Shelby. "Colly is with Gunther."

"What are you talking about, Jaz? You mean your friend from Yellowknife? That doesn't make any sense. Did you hit your head or something?"

"No," she said, "listen…"

George handed her the radio. "Jaz, Sergeant Sugar wants to talk to you."

"I'm here, Sergeant Sugar."

"Jaz, we're very glad we found you, and don't worry. With your help, Colly will be back safe real soon."

"Sergeant Sugar, there's more…"

"In a minute, Jaz. First let's figure out where Colly is."

He had Jaz unfurl the big white search map Shelby and George had with them. It was divided into squares. Jaz studied the map until she found the section where she thought they'd waited out the night, and then she followed her finger to the meeting spot on Blue Mountain.

"That's good, Jaz. We're sending help—to you and to Colly," Sergeant Sugar assured her. "There's heavy snow in Norman Wells right now. A helicopter will be out as soon as it clears, but we'll send a ground crew to Blue Mountain right now."

"How long before it gets there?"

"About an hour. Less if we can get the snowmobiles through."

"That's too long! Sergeant Sugar…there's more you need to know." As quickly as she could, she told him about Gunther, about the diamonds, and about the meeting that would take place in less than an hour. As she spoke, George and Shelby stared at her, mouths open.

She waited.

"Jaz." Sergeant Sugar's voice was soothing. Too soothing. "I need you to stay calm and let George and Shelby take care of you. Very soon we'll have you warmed up, and everything will be much clearer."

"But what about the Russians and Luka?"

"It's okay, Jaz. We'll look after everything from here. Now give the radio back to George, okay?"

She handed it to him, only half listening as Sergeant Sugar told George to stay put and to call him if Jaz showed any signs of distress.

Distress? She couldn't get any more distressed!

"Wilco, out," George said.

"I don't think he believed me."

"You're just cold," Shelby said. "I mean, you were out all night, even if you did build a fire. You did build a fire, didn't you?"

"Colly did," she said, feeling numb, and not just from the cold. "We stayed up all night trying to figure this out, and now…" She felt close to tears.

"There, you see? You're just tired—crazy tired."

"But it's the truth!" Jaz cried. How could she make them believe her? If only she had proof.

She slapped her hand to her head and then her pocket. "I can't believe I forgot!" Her exhaustion must be numbing her brain. She unzipped her pocket, unfolded Gunther's note, and placed the diamond carefully in the center of her palm. "It's one of the ones Gunther was supposed to give the mob. It has the Canadian Diamond mark, but it's really a blood diamond."

"Holy-moley," George said, whistling.

"You can say that again," Shelby said as she read the note.

"Holy-moley," George said again, shaking his head.

Shelby handed the note back to Jaz. "It'll be okay. When Sergeant Sugar gets here, you can give the note and the diamond to him. He'll see that you're telling the truth, and they'll go after these guys."

Jaz nodded. It made sense. But if it was so sensible, why did she feel so unsettled? A worry wiggled its way from her brain to her belly and twisted into a knot.

"I can't wait," she squeaked. "I've got to go back."

"What are you talking about, Jaz?" Shelby said. "You can't go back—it's too dangerous! Wait here and let Sergeant Sugar and the RCMP handle it."

"We can't wait! Colly and Gunther are on their way to Blue Mountain right now. What if something goes wrong? Lend me your dog team. If I leave right now, I can at least be there to…"

"To do what? It's too dangerous! Wait for Sergeant Sugar," Shelby said.

"No! Sergeant Sugar and the RCMP won't be able to make a plan in time. They'll only end up arguing and messing things up." Jaz was close to tears, but they were more from anger than fear. "All adults ever do is argue!"

Suddenly she wasn't sure if she was talking about Sergeant Sugar and the RCMP or her mom and dad. It didn't matter. It was always the same. She tilted her head back and let loose a big sound—half scream and half shout—from her belly. When she finished, she looked at her friends. Shelby looked slightly alarmed.

"Is this Gunther's?" George asked finally, reaching for the 30-30 rifle.

"Yes."

"I'll go with you," he said.

"Are you crazy?" Shelby screeched. "We're kids! What can we do against the Russian mob?"

"Maybe nothing, but Jaz is right. We have to go now. If we wait, we might be too late. Someone needs to be there…just in case."

"In case of what?" Shelby cried.

George just shrugged.

Relief mixed with hope and fear swirled through Jaz's body. It wouldn't fix anything, but it was better than sitting and waiting. She handed Gunther's note and the diamond to Shelby. "You stay here and give this to Sergeant Sugar."

"I think you're crazy to go back there, but if I can't stop you…" Shelby looked hopefully at George and Jaz, who were shaking their heads. "Fine. When Sergeant Sugar gets here, he'll know what to do."

Jaz nodded. "Thanks, Shelby." She turned to George. "Ready?"

"Let's go."

Chapter Thirteen

After crossing the Little Keele, their journey to Blue Mountain was slow because of tangled trees and the lack of a clear path, but there was none of the terror of the night before. No wolves howled from nearby trees.

"This is where we turned off to the shelter," Jaz said. "What time is it?"

"Eleven thirty."

"We're going to have to go fast if we're going to catch up. The main trail up the mountain should be faster."

Before they could climb the mountain, they had to get through a low area, thick with brush. It was slow going as they helped the dogs around tangles of willow and thick clumps of snow-laden alder. As they pushed on, chunks of soft snow dropped onto their shoulders and melted down their necks. In spite of the March sun shining from the now clear skies, and the warmth of exertion, Jaz was soon shivering.

After what felt like too long, the trail widened. The trees became straggly and short, and over their diminishing height, Jaz could see the barren top of Blue Mountain.

"George, I think we're almost there, but it doesn't look like we'll have cover for long. They'll see us coming."

"Why don't we leave the dogs here and see what's ahead?"

She nodded and helped George settle the dogs.

As they started up the more open trail, Jaz listened to the thumping of her heart.

Thwack, thwack, thwack. That wasn't her heart!

"George…"

"I hear it."

They backed into the brush as well as they could and scanned the sky, trying to peer around granite cliffs patched with snow, waiting for the helicopter to appear. It didn't, and after a while the thwacking sound ceased.

"What time is it?"

"Just about noon."

Her heart sank. If the helicopter had been the one Sergeant Sugar was sending, they would have seen it coming from behind them. No. If it was almost noon, it had to be the Russians!

"Let's climb to the top of that cliff," she said, pointing up. "We can see more from above."

Away from the shelter of brush, the path was an easy mix of gravel, snow and the odd clump of low bush and shrubs. As they reached their perch, sliding on their bellies to the edge, Jaz's heart almost stopped beating. They had a clear view of a plateau almost surrounded by crags like the one they'd just climbed. It looked like some sort of arena, with stands rising high on three sides. In the center of the snow-covered space there was a helicopter, with two men standing off to the side, their backs to George and Jaz. They were looking to the opening where the plateau sloped downward into trees and brush. From the brush, a dog team had just emerged.

"Holy-moley," George whispered.

Jaz held her breath as the two men walked out to meet the sled, which had stopped just beyond the trees. Colly stepped from the sled, package in hand.

"It doesn't look like Gunther is in very good shape, Jaz."

He was right. In the belly of the sled, Gunther was slumped over, not even watching. Beside her, George pulled out the 30-30 and aimed it into the clearing.

"What do you think you're doing?" she whispered.

"This is just in case," he whispered back. Despite his words, he didn't sound very sure. His voice was shaking, and he looked pale.

In the clearing, Colly was shouting something. She couldn't make out his words, but whatever they were, they didn't seem to bother the two men, who stood about twenty feet from the sled. One of the men shouted over his shoulder toward the helicopter. A third man emerged, dragging a small boy. Luka! His arms were bound, and it looked like there was a gag covering his mouth.

In the sled, Gunther was stirring. He lifted one arm, then slumped back down.

The man holding the boy stopped directly behind the other two. The boy fell to his knees but was yanked upright again by the man holding him. The first man waved his arms and shouted at Colly. Colly held the package straight in front and shouted back. What was he arguing about? This was so NOT a good time to argue.

Bzzzzzzz…

Jaz looked over her shoulder. "George, I hear snowmobiles."

Of all the worst possible timing! She glanced back into the clearing and immediately ducked, as everyone except Gunther and Luka were looking their way. They'd heard the snowmobiles too.

George poked her. "It's the rangers!" From the path where they'd left the dogs, three snowmobiles emerged, each one driven by a man wearing the telltale vibrant red ballcap of the Canadian Rangers. Jaz knew that under their parkas, each also wore a matching red sweatshirt. One ranger stopped and got off his snowmobile, while the other two continued along the tree line.

"They have no idea what they're heading into!" Jaz groaned.

"No, but look!" George replied.

In the clearing, the helicopter started up again. The waving man shouted at Colly, and the man holding Luka shook the small boy. Whatever Colly's argument had been, he'd apparently decided to give it up. He tossed the package. The waving man snatched it and sprinted back toward the helicopter, which looked ready to lift off. The two men with him followed...with Luka!

"We have to do something!" Jaz shouted, no longer caring if they were heard. "Why are they taking Luka?"

"Hostage, I expect…Jaz…I don't know what to do."

"Shoot at something!"

"I don't know what to shoot at. I can't shoot a person!"

George had gone from pale to gray to a kind of green around the edges. "Fine," Jaz said. "Give it to me."

As soon as she held the rifle in her hands, she began to understand what George meant. This was real and those were real people, bad or not.

Her brain in overdrive, Jaz scanned the clearing. "We need a diversion, George, and fast."

Below them, Luka was causing problems for the man holding him; he fell to the ground, kicking, making it hard for the man to hold on to him.

"There!" George said, pointing toward a large overhang of snow on the edge of a nearby crag. "Shoot that."

She pointed the rifle toward it, flipped off the safety and squeezed.

Crack!

The force of the shot punched the butt of the rifle back into her shoulder, and she reeled over in pain. She'd forgotten about the recoil! Groaning, she peered at where she'd shot. Nothing. The snow stayed in place. She'd hoped it would fall, maybe create a snowslide. She must have missed.

It did cause a reaction though. In the clearing, the men had dropped to their bellies. Colly was waving toward Luka, and the boy began rolling, arms still bound, toward the sled.

Suddenly there was shouting. Lots of shouting!

The rangers burst through the trees into the clearing, jumped off their snowmobiles and crouched behind them. They aimed their rifles at the helicopter, where one man, now sitting, had his arms up high. The man who had been holding Luka was on his knees, hands also above his head. The third man, the one who had taken the package of diamonds, stood up with a pistol in his hand. He didn't look like he was about to give up any time soon.

She looked frantically for Luka, and then she spotted his tiny foot disappearing behind the sled. Good. He was hiding. But what about Colly? Jaz stopped breathing. He was still standing by the sled.

There was more shouting, and slowly the man

with the pistol backed toward the helicopter. The other two men followed while the rangers watched, unmoving. Colly stayed frozen in place. The men pulled themselves into the helicopter just as it lifted off.

It was as if someone had suddenly hit "Play." Colly threw himself behind the sled with Luka, while the rangers raced along the edge of the trees and found new places to take aim at the helicopter.

"We've got to hide!" Jaz shouted at George, suddenly feeling very exposed.

As the helicopter rose above them, Jaz could see the whites of very surprised-looking eyes staring back at her. Then they were gone again as the helicopter disappeared.

The ranger who had stopped by the sled was jogging upslope toward them. He was talking into a handheld radio.

Suddenly Jaz heard the return of the helicopter's *thwap, thwap, thwap* and looked up in terror.

"It's okay, Jaz. It's the search helicopter," George said, one hand on her arm.

A blue and red helicopter emerged from the direction of the Little Keele. It flew over their heads and landed in the clearing.

It was going to be okay. The diamond thieves had gotten away, but Luka was safe, and Jaz and her friends were all alive. Or were they? Except for when he first saw Luka, Gunther hadn't moved.

Chapter Fourteen

"We didn't exactly have a choice, sir," Jaz cried.

Their rescue had been swift. An unconscious Gunther had been placed on a stretcher and sent to Yellowknife for emergency medical care. Luka had also been taken to Yellowknife, where he had been reunited with his mother. Jaz, Colly and George had returned to Norman Wells. Now she and Colly were seated at a camp table, facing a very stern Sergeant Sugar.

"I understand that, up to a point. Colly, you took a terrible risk going with Gunther up the mountain. And you, Jaz...I hardly know where to begin."

"But..."

"No buts, Jaz. Beyond what did happen, and what might have happened, you should not have set off alone on foot. I know you've only been with the unit for a few months, but you should know we put you in pairs for a reason."

"So that we learn to get along?" Jaz asked hopefully. She turned and high-fived Colly, who high-fived her back.

"No, though I'm glad to see you've worked on that. Colly, would you like to tell Jaz why I'm so upset with you both?"

"Because we split up," he said, head down.

Jaz opened her mouth to protest, but she was interrupted by a commotion outside the door.

"I told you that I don't care. If you can't keep her safe…"

"Mom!" Jaz cried and raced to the tent flap just as it opened and her mother and father rushed in. They were immediately followed by Colly's uncle.

Hugs, and tears from her mother, were over quickly as Sergeant Sugar cleared his throat. "Folks, I know we have a lot to talk about, but if you wouldn't mind waiting just a bit, we have an awards ceremony to see to."

A tiny ember of hope burned in her belly. "Did we win the derby, Sergeant Sugar? We were way ahead of everyone else!"

"No, Jaz."

The ember snuffed out.

"You didn't win, but every patrol in this derby dropped everything to search for you. Don't you want to show your appreciation?"

"But if they dropped everything, how do you know who won?"

"We've worked out every team's time up until we stopped the race."

She knew it was wrong to be disappointed, but she couldn't help it. She'd wanted so badly to win. Instead of making her mom and dad proud, she'd landed herself in a dangerous situation. Again.

As they grouped into their patrols on the snow-covered parade grounds by the shore of the Mackenzie River, Colly bumped up beside her. "Your mom sounded pretty mad."

"Yeah, she's always mad lately, mostly at my dad."

"Why?"

She sighed. "She wants me to go live with her in Edmonton."

"Do you want to?"

"It's not that I don't want to." She frowned. "Actually, no, I don't want to. I like it in Destiny. I only wish I could see her more."

"Why don't you just tell her?"

Tweet!

A whistle blast told the patrols to stand at attention. As Jaz moved into place, Colly added, "For what it's worth, I'd like you to stay in Destiny too, Jaz." He jabbed her with his elbow. "But sheesh, you could start listening to people who outrank you."

Seeing his smirk, she grinned and jabbed him back. "I will when they start listening to me!"

Tweet! *Tweet*!

Sergeant Sugar was standing directly in front of them. "Colly, Jaz, if you are ready, we'd like to begin the awards."

"Ready, Sergeant Sugar!" Colly said, snapping to attention.

"Jaz?"

"Did we win after all?"

"Jaz!"

"Okay, just kidding."

The cheers were deafening as Major Chris announced each winner. First place went to a team from Fort Resolution Patrol. Second went to a pair from Tuktoyaktuk. As third place was announced, Jaz cheered loudest of all. It was Shelby and George!

As the winning teams stood tall and received

their medals, Major Chris stepped back up to the microphone. "You are all a credit to the JCRs, and I am very proud of each of you. The Northwest Territories Junior Canadian Rangers will be well represented during the Canada Day celebrations in Ottawa!"

He waited while the crowd erupted into wild cheering. He held up his hand, and the crowd hushed. "We're not quite finished yet. As you know, we had some unexpected excitement during our race."

Jaz could feel everyone turn and look at her and Colly.

"On occasion, it is our great privilege to honor JCRs who have shown extreme courage in difficult situations. JCR Jaz and Master Corporal Colly from Destiny Patrol—will you come forward, please?"

Her heart was racing as she stepped to the stage and stood at attention beside Colly.

"Sometimes we find ourselves in extreme situations that no one can predict. In this situation, though your own lives were in danger, you worked together, showing incredible courage. You also saved a man's life and helped rescue a little boy. That, I know, is reward in itself, but I am very pleased to tell you that you have each been recommended to receive the Medal of Bravery."

Jaz looked into the cheering crowd and saw her mom and dad beaming at her. With the ceremony finished, she leapt from the stage and into their arms. Major Chris joined them, along with an RCMP officer. "Jaz, congratulations again."

"Thank you, Major Chris."

"This is Corporal Johnny Lu from the Yellowknife RCMP Diamond Squad. He'd like to talk to you when you have a moment—you and Colly."

Worried, she looked up at the RCMP officer. "Have we done something wrong?"

The man laughed. "No, you're not in trouble, but when you and your parents are ready, I'll need a statement from you."

"What's going to happen to Gunther, sir?"

"Gunther is in trouble, there is no doubt about that. But his cooperation should work in his favor."

"What if the diamond thieves come after him—or Luka—again?"

"You'll be happy to hear that the men who kidnapped Luka have been arrested. Beyond that, we will do our best to make sure Gunther's family is safe."

After promising to give her statement soon, it was time to face the music. The *real* music. She turned to her parents. "Mom and Dad, I'm sorry about everything that happened. I guess you're mad, huh?"

Her mom had tears in her eyes. So did her dad.

"Jaz," her mom said. "What are we going to do with you?"

She sniffled. "I don't know, Mom. Things just kind of happen to me."

"I know they do, sweetheart. I can see that."

"But, Mom…" She stopped. How could she say what she really needed to say, especially when she knew it would make her mom sad?

No, Colly was right. It was best to be honest, even with the stuff that was hard to say. She just needed to find the right way to say it. "Mom, I love you so much, and I want to see you more. But…"

"What is it, sweetheart?" In spite of the question, it looked like Mom knew. It also looked like she was about to burst into tears.

Taking a deep breath, she tried again. "Mom, I really like living in Destiny, and I love being a JCR. I love ice crystals and northern lights and having caribou practically in my backyard. I even love wolves, even though I don't ever want to get close to one again."

Her mom closed her eyes and squeezed Jaz's hands. Jaz gulped. She had to finish.

"Mom…I'd like you to visit more, but I really want to stay with Dad."

After a moment, her mother opened her eyes. She wasn't crying, though her eyes were red around the rims. "Are you sure, Jaz? It's just that I get so worried about you. And it's not just me. Your dad worries too."

Dad nodded.

"I know you worry. I don't know how to stop that, but I'm learning lots with the Junior Rangers, stuff that will help keep me safe."

"It's okay, Jaz," Dad said. "We're your parents. We're supposed to worry. That doesn't stop no matter where we are, and no matter what you are doing or how old you are."

"We are also very proud of you, hon," Mom said, tearful again. "Do you know that?"

Jaz felt her insides begin to glow. "Does that mean you're okay with me staying in Destiny?"

"Yes, I guess I am. You're a northern girl, through and through. I can see that now. I'm not. I do like to visit though. Maybe I can visit more often."

"Does this mean you'll stop arguing with Dad?"

"Let me take this one," Dad said. "Jaz, I didn't even know it bothered you. I'm sorry. I'm sure your mom is too."

"Yes, I am, sweetheart. We'll do better, okay?"

Jaz nodded. "Maybe I can visit you more often in Edmonton. Would that help?"

He mother smiled. "Yes, it would. Very much."

"Dad? What do you say?"

"Well, Jaz, I guess I'd say..." He put his hands on his hips and scowled as if he was angry. Then he laughed and winked. "I just happen to know someone with an airplane."

"Well, great," Jaz said, grinning. "That makes it simple, and you know how much I like things nice and simple."

She hooted with laughter and ducked as something whizzed by her ear. Who knew her mom threw such a mean snowball?

Anita Daher began her life in a small town on Prince Edward Island, but left at the age of five, remaining something of a gypsy ever since. Many of her favorite childhood memories involve roaming over rocks by Hudson Bay and fishing on the tundra in the Northwest Territories. Her writing reflects the places she's been blessed to spend time in. Earlier thrillers for young readers are *Flight from Big Tangle* and *Flight from Bear Canyon* (Orca). Anita lives in Winnipeg, Manitoba, with her husband, two daughters, one basset hound and a Westfalia camper van named Mae.

Other books by Anita Daher

Diamond Willow Award nominee 2004

Lost in the forest as a fire rages, Kaylee finds her way home, only to discover she must overcome her fear of flying and pilot a floatplane to safety.

Flight from Big Tangle
978-1-55143-234-2

Other books by Anita Daher

Our Choice 2005

In this sequel to Flight from Big Tangle, *Kaylee must fly a plane for a second time, this time to rescue Jack, who has crashed his helicopter near a group of grizzlies.*

Flight from Bear Canyon
978-1-55143-326-4

Recent Orca Young Readers

Tall tales help Eddie understand the world.

The Big Snapper

Katherine Holubitsky

978-1-55143-563-3

Yossi dreams of playing hockey—but he has no skates.

Yossi's Goal

Ellen Schwartz

978-1-55143-492-6

Recent Orca Young Readers

Will the secret signs lead Henry to his father?

Secret Signs

Jacqueline Guest

978-1-55143-599-2